# Three Sisters

## Audrey Wood

PICTURES BY

## Rosekrans Hoffman

Dial easy-to-read

DIAL BOOKS FOR YOUNG READERS · New York

*For the two,*
*Jennifer and Edwina*
A.W.

*For Jessy and James Charles*
R.H.

Published by Dial Books for Young Readers
2 Park Avenue
New York, New York 10016

Published simultaneously in Canada by
Fitzhenry & Whiteside Limited, Toronto

Library of Congress Cataloging-in-Publication Data
Wood, Audrey. Three sisters.
*Summary:* A frolicsome trio of sisters twirl their way
through three escapades involving speaking "French,"
dancing lessons, and their uncle's annoying cigars.
[1. Sisters—Fiction.]
I. Hoffman, Rosekrans, ill. II. Title.
PZ7.W846Th 1986 [E] 85-29392
ISBN 0-8037-0279-5
ISBN 0-8037-0280-9 (lib. bdg.)

First Edition
W
10 9 8 7 6 5 4 3 2 1

The full-color artwork was prepared using pencil,
colored pencils, and colored inks.
It was then camera-separated and reproduced
as red, blue, yellow, and black halftones.

Reading Level 2.0

# Contents

# PINKY SPEAKS FRENCH

Pinky's sisters were at the mirror.

"Zee voo wah-la!" said Babs.

"We are speaking French."

"You can't speak French!" said Pinky.

"We're making our words
*sound* French," said Babs.
"We can fool everyone."
"Poor lay voo, ooo-eee," said Dot.
"Aren't we smart and fancy?"

"I want to speak French too,"
said Pinky.
"No, no, Pinky dear," said Dot.
"Speaking French is for big girls."

"We are off to the ice cream shop,"
said Babs.

"Speaking French no matter what."

"I want to go too," said Pinky.

"No way!" said Babs.

"You would ruin everything."

"Ta-ta Pinky-voo," said Dot.

"Ta-ta Pinky-voo," said Babs.

The two sisters walked down the street.

Pinky followed.

"Hello, girls," a lady said to

Dot and Babs.

"Do you know the time?"

"Me clocky no lay vooz," said Babs.

"Bon-bon, Madame," said Dot.

"Oh, my!" the lady said.

"You must be from another country."

The two sisters walked on.

"Did you see that lady's face?"

whispered Dot.

"It was *too* funny," whispered Babs.

"What a scream!"

Dot and Babs kept speaking French.

At last they came

to the ice cream shop.

"Gross!" said Babs.

"Spud and Eddie are here."

The boys waved at them.

"Let's go home," said Dot.

"We can't," said Babs.

"They saw us."

"Spud and Eddie make me shy,"
said Dot.

"Me too," said Babs.

"But don't let them know it."

"I won't let them know it," said Dot.

"I won't let them know it either,"
said Babs.

The sisters walked past Spud and
Eddie without saying hello.

They sat in a booth nearby.

"Eee-eee, ooo-ooo." The boys
made monkey noises at the sisters.

They flew paper airplanes at
Babs and Dot.

"I hate this," whispered Dot.

"I know!" whispered Babs.

"Still it is kind of fun."

"We could ask the boys to share a banana split," said Dot.

"I dare you to ask," said Babs.

"I double dare you to ask," said Dot.

"I bet you won't do it," said Babs.

"I bet you won't do it too," said Dot.

Just then Pinky skipped into the shop.

"Boo-boo bon zooey!" said Pinky.

"What did she say?" asked Eddie.

"Voo la-la," said Pinky.

The boys looked at Babs and Dot.

"Who is she?" Spud asked.

"I don't know her," said Babs.

"I don't know her either," said Dot.

"I know who she is," said Eddie.

"That's your little sister."

"Ooo-eee toodle-ooo!" said Pinky.

"Non zoo booey!"

"Wow!" said Spud.

"Where did she learn to talk
like that?" asked Eddie.
"I am speaking French," said Pinky.
"I learned it from Babs and Dot."
The boys started to laugh.
They couldn't stop.

"I could just die!" said Dot.

"I could just die too!" said Babs.

"Let's get out of here."

Babs and Dot ran out of the shop.

"You sure have crazy sisters," said Spud.

"Bon-bon," said Pinky.

"Bon-bon."

# DOT LIKES TO DANCE

Dot put on her new dance outfit.

"Today I take my first dance lesson,"
she said.

"I will learn to be a ballerina."

"Will you be famous?" asked Pinky.

"Of course Dot will be famous,"
said Babs.

"I will tell her what to do."

"Everyone will be happy when I dance," said Dot.

"I will dance for joy and never get tired."

"I will have Dot dance for the queen," said Babs.

"And the prince will sit with me!"

"I will wear a white gown," said Dot.

"Everyone will send me flowers."

"They will want to meet me,"

said Babs, "because I have

a famous sister."

"Wow-eee!" said Pinky.

Babs put on the music.

"Now I will dance for you," said Dot.

She danced like a leaf in the wind.

She danced like a fawn in the woods.

She danced like a flame on a candle.

"Bravo! Bravo!" the sisters cheered.

Pinky and Babs went

to Dot's dance lesson.

They waited in the hall.

At last Dot came out. She looked sad.

"I hated it," said Dot.

"The teacher made us stand in a line.

Then she made us do steps.

Toe in, toe out.

Toe in, toe out."

"Yick!" said Pinky.

"Why did you do that?"

"That's how ballerinas learn

to dance," said Dot.

"The teacher said so."

The sisters walked sadly home.

Dot flopped on the sofa.

"Now I know," she said.

"I will never be a ballerina.

I am not going back."

"Rats!" said Babs.

"Now the prince won't sit with me."

"I will miss your dancing,"
said Pinky.

"It was kind of nice," said Babs.

"I was never sad when I danced,"
said Dot.

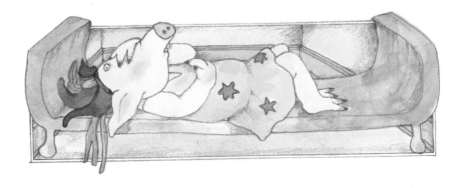

Dot put on the music.

She danced like a leaf in the wind.

She danced like a fawn in the woods.

She danced like a flame on a candle.

"Bravo! Bravo!" the sisters cheered.

# BABS AND THE CIGAR

"Uncle George is here to baby-sit,"
Dot called.

"P.U. cigars!" Babs cried.

"I hate his cigars!" said Dot.
"They smell like bad cheese."

"I won't let Uncle George smoke cigars," said Babs.

"You can't stop him," said Pinky.

"Just wait and see," said Babs.

The sisters found their uncle

reading the newspaper.

"Hello, girls," he said.

"The moon is out.

Let's go for a stroll."

"I think we don't like

moonlight strolls," Babs said.

She flipped on the TV.

Uncle George took out a cigar.

It was wrapped in clear plastic.

"Ahhh," he said.

Dot poked Babs in the ribs.

"P.U.," she whispered.

"We will soon smell a cigar."

Babs reached under the table and
knocked three times.

"What was that?" asked Uncle George.

"I think someone is at the door,"
said Babs.

Uncle George went to see.

The sisters looked at the cigar.

"Don't touch it!" said Pinky.

Babs picked up the cigar.

She acted like she was smoking.

"P.U. cigars!" Dot and Pinky cried.

The sisters heard heavy footsteps.

Babs hid the cigar in the flower pot.

"That's odd," Uncle George said.

"No one was at the door."

He looked around.

"That's double odd," he said.

"I've lost my cigar."

Uncle George searched his pockets.

He pulled out another cigar and
tore off the plastic.

"Ahhh," he said.

He opened a box of matches.

"For sure," whispered Dot.

"We will now smell a cigar."

"Stop!" Babs shouted.

"Don't light that cigar!"

"Why not?" asked Uncle George.

"I'll light it for you," said Babs.

Babs took the matches.

"But first I must feed the fish,"
she said.

Babs went to the fish bowl.

She fed the fish.

She dropped the matches in the fish bowl.

"Oh, no!" cried Babs.

"The matches are wet!

Now you can't smoke a cigar!"

"No problem," said Uncle George.

He took out his lighter.

At last Uncle George lit his cigar.

"Ahhh," he said.

"I knew you couldn't stop him,"

whispered Dot.

"I'm dying," whispered Babs.

"That cigar smoke is killing me!"

Babs acted like she was choking.

She fell across her sister's lap.

"Here are my last words,"

she whispered.

Dot and Pinky leaned down to hear.

"P.U. cigars!"

Dot and Pinky began to giggle.

They laughed until their sides ached.

"What's so funny?"

asked Uncle George.

"Say it, Babs," Pinky said.

"Say it, Babs," Dot said.

Babs looked at Uncle George.

"P.U. cigars," she said.

Uncle George was surprised.

"You were laughing at me," he said.

The girls felt bad.

"Babs made us laugh," said Dot.

"Dot and Pinky made me say it,"

said Babs.

"I guess my cigar is smelly,"
Uncle George said.

"I won't smoke it anymore."
Uncle George put down the cigar.

He looked at it sadly and sighed.

"We're sorry we were so mean,"
said Dot.

"I know what!" said Babs.
"Let's go for a moonlit stroll."

"Ahhh, yes," said Uncle George.
And the four strolled out
into the moonlight.